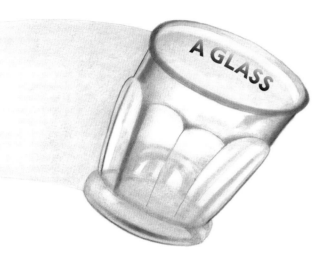

Creative Editions

A GLASS

Etienne   Delessert

A glass. A simple glass, full of memories.

I met my mother when I was 2 1/2.

   She had been a teacher, and my father hired her to take loving care of me. My birth mother had died after I was born.

   I can still see the scene the first time we met. The glossy gray door and the round brass handle. We were both intimidated, but she saw that I focused on a little duck pin on her dark red sweater.

She offered it to me. Her name was Eglantine Besson.

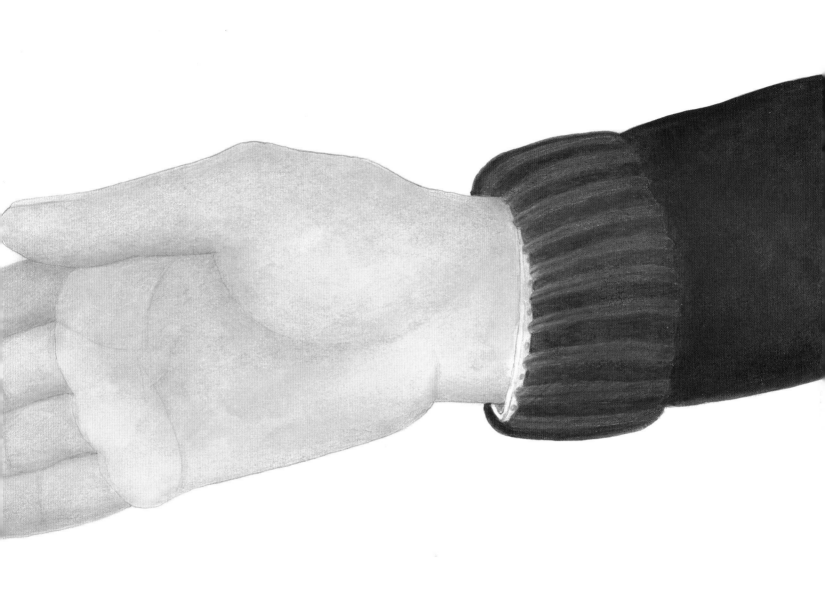

In forest hammocks, M'zelle Besson told me stories about kingfishers, wild mushrooms, and roaring monsters.

We picked strawberries which she cooked into jams in a deep copper pot. We took snails for rides around the garden in my wooden carriage. We staged plays. The characters we invented are still alive today in my stories.

She married my father, a Protestant minister, when I was 7. All my friends wanted a mom just like mine.

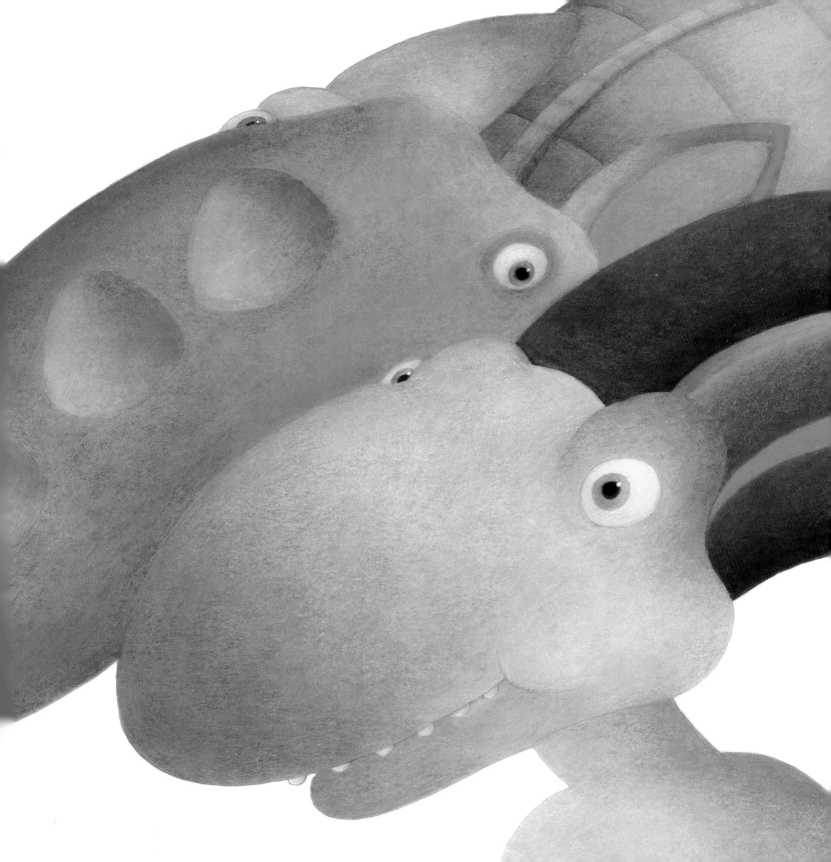

Only twice did my mother and I truly fight.

Once, I was 14 and wanted to stop taking piano lessons from Mademoiselle Bach, my stern teacher. My mother said, NO!

So I told her that *she was not my real mother.*

It made her cry.

The other time, I was 21, and we were standing in the kitchen. I can't even remember the reason for her anger, but she threw a heavy crystal glass at me!

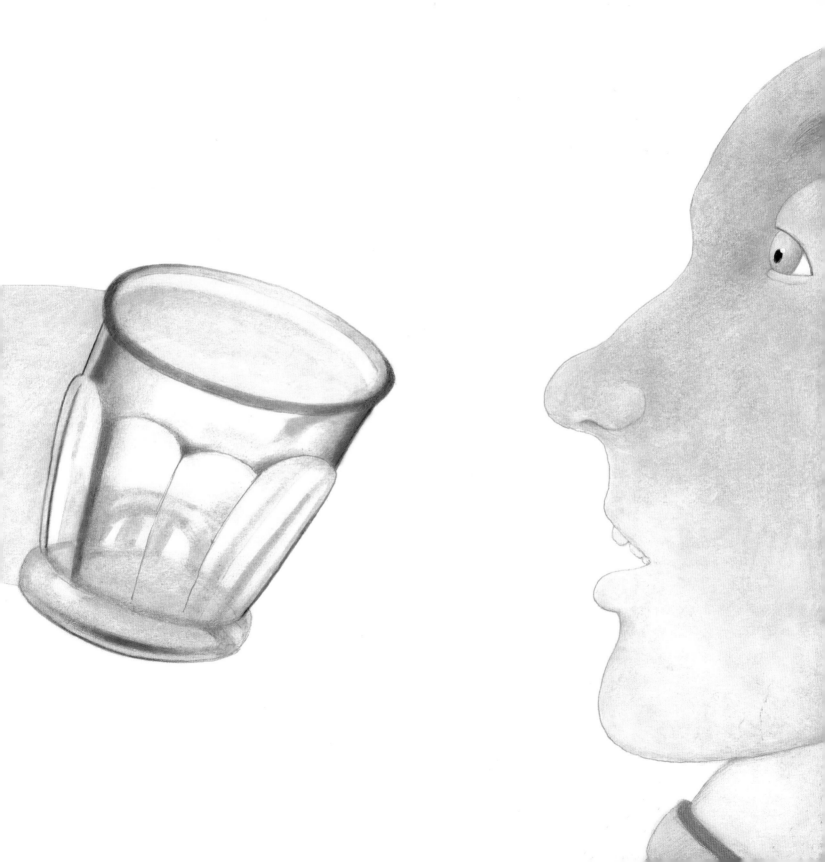

The glass missed me, hit a wall, bounced on the floor, and ended up against another wall.
    It did not break.

We laughed, hugged ...
for the rest of her long life.

That very glass now sits on my drawing table, among watercolor paints, brushes, color pencils, feathers, and toys. Light sparkles through it. I think of my mother.

She could be here, a presence looking over my shoulder.

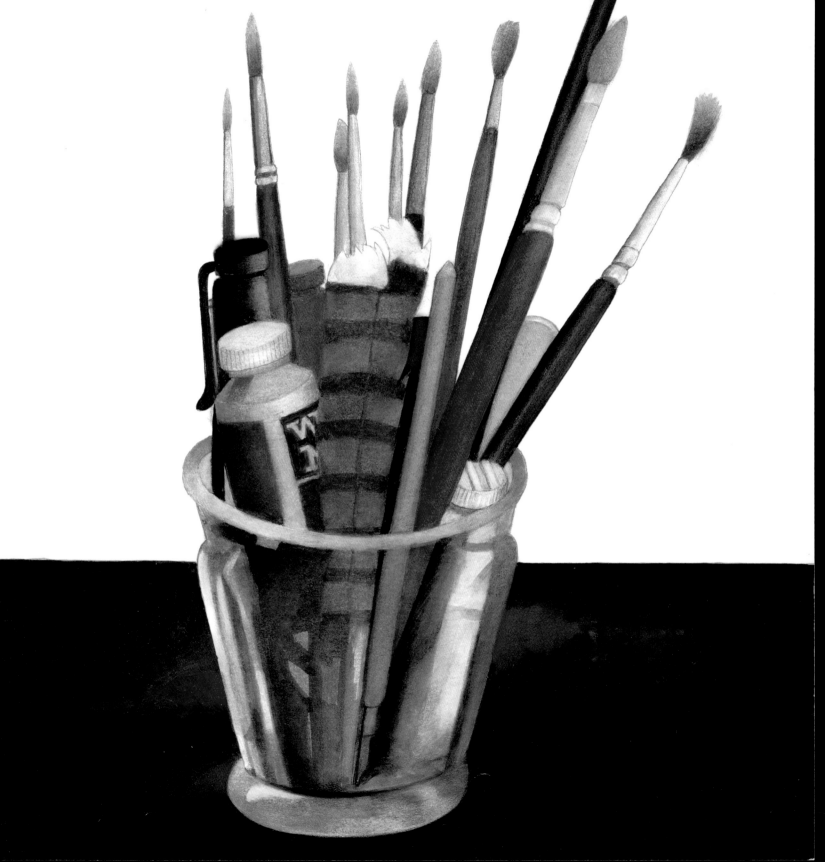

My mom loved books—a love she passed on to me. She enjoyed nonsense poems, cartoons, historical novels, and detective stories.

She was an ace at crossword puzzles.

After my father died and I moved to America, she visited me in New York and, later, in the rolling hills of Connecticut, where I now live with my wife Rita.

Since our young son did not speak French then, she felt that I had robbed her of being a grandmother.

I worried she was right.

Eglantine lived to be 92. Until the end, she relished smoking little cigars.

She was an Aquarius—only air and water. I am a Capricorn—earth and fire. Perhaps our lives were written together in the stars.

She was my *real* mom.

Text and illustrations copyright © 2013 Etienne Delessert
Published in 2013 by Creative Editions
P.O. Box 227, Mankato, MN 56002 USA
Creative Editions is an imprint of The Creative Company.
Designed by Rita Marshall. Edited by Aaron Frisch.
Printed in China.
Library of Congress Cataloging-in-Publication Data
This book has been submitted to the Library of Congress for CIP data processing.
Data is available at http://catalog.loc.gov/. LCCN: 2012051632.
ISBN 978-1-56846-257-8

First Edition
2 4 6 8 9 7 5 3 1